Twinbridge

A Novella

by

Catherine Mathews

Copyright © 2018 by Catherine Mathews

All rights reserved.

ISBN: 1717254497
ISBN-13: 978-1717254498

Twinbridge depicts life in a small New England town in mid-twentieth century America during the Great Depression and World War Two.

Dear Elke,
 May you enjoy this fictionalized version of life in small-town America during the Depression and War!
  Catherine
   January, 2019

I dedicate this book to St. Francis Church;
To clergy and members, past and present,
whose spiritual, social and practical support,
so generously given,
have made the writing of it possible.

I thank the following:

Catherine Lewis, Dorothy Spruzen, and Pat Atkisson; who besides being wonderful writers themselves, are gifted in the art of editing and in offering suggestions of paths to be explored.

Kristin Clark Taylor, the founder of the Great Falls Writer's Group, who makes all want-to-be writers feel they can do the impossible,

Myrna Stuart, whose encouragement has meant much,

Bill Lewers, who, with his books, has led by example, and

Lynn Fallon, my editor, who has organized the final effort and helped me across the finish line.

Part One

Twinbridge Present (1975)..1

Part Two

Twinbridge Remembered (1943-1945)

    Chapters:

    One – Getting Acquainted..13

    Two – The New Teacher..25

    Three – Trip to Ransom 35

    Four – Saturday Night 45

    Five – The New York Times 57

    Six – The Christmas Locket......................................65

    Seven – The Davis Place 71

    Eight – Mrs. Cartwright's Library 83

    Nine – The Telephone Company 91

Ten – James' Graduation 101

Eleven – Off To War 107

Twelve – Lindsey's Letter 113

Thirteen – Listening In 117

Fourteen – A Visit 127

Fifteen – Change of Plans 137

Sixteen – More Change of Plans 147

Seventeen – At The Farm 155

Eighteen – Lindsey's Parents 165

Nineteen – Fire 171

Twenty – Change of Heart 181

Part Three
Twinbridge Farewell (1975) 187

Part One

Twinbridge Present

1975

Lindsey wakened to a persistent clicking sound; rolling over she saw it came from a clock standing on the white-painted mantel, the sort of collectible to which B&B owners were partial. The August sun filtered through the leaves outside the window. She buried her head under the quilt, trying to recapture sleep, but now she was entirely awake.

She slid out of bed and dressed herself quickly in the early morning chill, splashing water on her face from the sink in the corner of the room. She pulled a sweater from her suitcase and threw it around her shoulders.

The house was silent as she made her way quietly down the curving stair to the kitchen entrance, unlatched the door and stepped into the garden. She shivered and pulled the sweater more tightly around her. Early morning in New England already warned of approaching fall.

It was Sunday; she was the only one about. All the better for re-visiting. She walked swiftly, a short block on Church Street to the bridge. She paused for a moment after she passed the White Church. The small square of open land adjoining it could hardly be called a park, though obviously that had been the intention. A plaque set on a post near the sidewalk read, "In memory of Twinbridge School, built 1904." The footprint of the school was barely visible. Two benches faced each other in front of a neglected garden, their pock-marked varnished slats speaking of long exposure to hard winters, the back of one leaning at an awkward angle.

It doesn't look as if anyone ever sits there. In another ten years no one will remember.

She continued the few steps further to the top of the bridge that tipped downward toward the town. From there she looked across Main Street to see the Town Hall with Doc Edmunds' fine brick house to its left. She was amused to see that a foot path still cut diagonally across Dr. Edmunds' lawn just as it had when she and her parents had lived on the narrow road beyond. For those homeward bound from town to their homes on the hill above the Town Hall it was far easier to cut across Doc Edmunds' property than to walk to the corner and up the street. An unfamiliar square white building sat at the corner; the flag in front told her it was the post office. It took her a minute to realize what else was different about her family's house, tucked above it. The linden tree at their front step was there no longer. How plain their house looked without its great sheltering branches.

Lindsey started to walk down the bridge. To her left, below, lay the neat beige stucco building that had been the phone company. It looked precisely the same, unchanged but for the missing telephone sign. Two bicycles lay propped against the porch, and the remains of a basketball hoop hung on a post. It was a private home now, and a snug one, no doubt.

As the sun rose higher it lit up the dark roofs of the lower town. She rounded the corner to the right at the foot of the bridge to continue on Main Street.

The town of Twinbridge lay around her, familiar yet different. Lindsey recalled the unrelenting cold of those wartime winters twenty-five years ago—the crunch of crusted snow underfoot, the glitter of icy prisms on the streetlights, the weight of coats, scarves, gloves, hats, mittens, boots, all the winter paraphernalia. She smiled as she remembered. Where was summer in her memories? Why did it play the smaller part?

The sidewalk curved past the Block, the apartment building that hung out over the river, to pass the mill. She looked for the sprawling canvas sacks of feed that used to be left by the trucks against the big double doors, but the clutter of a working mill had stilled. The broad opening had been replaced by a single door with a curtained window, which sported a hand-painted sign, 'Gilman's Antiques.' Gone was the smell of freshly ground grain as it spilled from the machines beyond the open doors, and the sight of pale straw spread underfoot in the dusky interior.

Lindsey turned her attention to the old two-story building across the street. It had been a hotel, largely unoccupied during the war years, its lobby dusty and silent; a leftover from the days of traveling salesmen. A colonnade at street level sheltered the drug store, the jewelry store, and a pawn shop. She saw a sign at the end of the building, "Washington Apartments."

Farther down Main Street, she peered through the plate glass window of Hedley's Grocery. The old counter remained in place, but the shelves behind it with bags and boxes of groceries were gone. Two large aluminum coffee pots sat on the end of the counter with stacks of paper cups propped beside them. Several tables filled the room, with empty chairs parked haphazardly around them. On the door was a sign, 'Open at 5:00 p.m.' She stepped back to read the fat, brightly-colored letters arced across the top of the window, "Theodorakis Pizza Parlor."

A stand-alone building next door that had been Abbot's Department Store was freshly painted a dark green, as it had been years before. She and her mother had been frequent visitors there in those years when her mother sewed clothes for her. One of the items they had brought with them from Jersey was her mother's Singer sewing machine. Together at Abbot's they went through the Vogue pattern books, and scrutinized the few pieces of material. The tissue-paper patterns would be pinned to the material on the dining room table, the pieces finally cut. They would make a place for the sewing machine at one end of the table where her mother would work, pressing her knee against the lever, watching the moving lines of stitches under the light of the machine.

She remembered, too, the special excursion to Abbot's for the purchase of the teal-colored coat that replaced her worn jacket. Even her dad had accompanied them, to give his opinion, since it was a major expenditure. How she had loved that coat!

She wondered at the number of fat-bellied TV sets squatting in the show windows, and the lack of items of clothing. Then she noted the wooden sign above the top step, "Abbot's TV Services: Sales and Repair."

Across from Abbot's the window from the old post office still overlooked Main Street. She could make out some tables inside, and outside a sign, "Elton's Ice Cream Parlor."

From here she was able to see the library. It had a new sign on a post out front, but the painted red brick building was as it had been. The cement pathway led to the two steps up to the heavy door. The same brass doorknob hung in the center of the door. She was pleased to see that it had withstood change. She had had so many visits there during her high school journey, always leaving wiser than when she entered.

Stepping away from Abbot's, Lindsey was in front of the railroad station. The sidewalk here crumbled away to the side, dipping toward the parking area that adjoined the tracks. She slowed her steps. The brass railing still edged the sidewalk. She reached out to run her hand along its smooth surface. She was reminded of those sweet days when she first became aware of James. He had been leaning right there, waiting, looking for her. And she had been watching for him, more than twenty-five years ago, a young girl looking for love.

Part Two

Twinbridge Remembered

1943-1945

Chapter One

Getting Acquainted

Lindsey had never taken much notice of James Furling when she was a sophomore, during her first year in Twinbridge High School. Her family was in Twinbridge because of the war. Her dad could no longer sell used cars, as he had when they had first moved to Vermont from New Jersey. The car market disappeared after the war started, just as his stockbroker business in New York had failed after

1929. By 1943 with factories concentrating on war production no new cars were being made. People hung on to their old models. Consequently garages were busy, keeping the old cars running. Her dad was a good bookkeeper; he found a job keeping books in Ed Sherman's Chevy dealership in Twinbridge. He sold their family car; they didn't need it. They rented a house in town, just off Main Street. He walked to the dealership, which was on the road out of town on the way to Ransom. The school was even closer, just over the bridge; Lindsey was able to go home to lunch.

James, a junior, was just another of the half-grown farm boys, hunched over his books, mouthing the words to himself as he studied, blushing whenever anyone spoke to him. But in September, at the start of her junior year, and he was a senior, she saw how much he had changed. During the short months of summer he had suddenly grown taller, and the increased breadth of his shoulders strained his last year's jacket.

The Furling farm was at the other end of town, beyond the lower bridge, a walkable distance, but too far for James to go for the lunch recess. Like the students who came by bus, he brought a sandwich to eat at his desk. The grade school had their rooms on the first floor of the big square building; the four high school classes each had a corner room on the floor above. When the students finished their lunches, they emptied out into the large central halls. The younger children were forbidden to get near the banisters of the stairwells, but on the second floor; the older students leaned against the wide railings, free to do as they chose before the bell rang for afternoon classes.

    Lindsey, returning from home at noon, entered the school from the main door on Church Street and made her way to the stairs through the younger children on the first floor. She paused to give Gimpy an ear rub. The orange cat, in his usual spot on the ledge near the floor radiator, rose and arched his back, stretching fore and aft. It was Lindsey's habit to greet Gimpy when she entered the school. Meeting Gimpy had made Lindsey feel at home when she first came to Twinbridge. With her dad always looking for a job they had moved every year or every other year, ever since they had left Jersey. Sometimes they even moved in the middle of the school year. Lindsey was used to feeling like an outsider. Twinbridge was different, maybe because, not having a car, they lived in town. She got to know Barbara, who lived right across the street from the school. But before Barbara became her best friend there was Gimpy.

A homeless kitten, Gimpy had elected himself the school cat several years before Lindsey moved to Twinbridge. The school was having a mouse problem, so Jud Kenney, the janitor, left him in the basement at night, free to roam the school. Jud was a laconic character, moving into middle age, not known for talking unless he had something particular to say. He had had polio which left him with one leg shorter than the other, he wore a steel brace. He was exempted from military service, of course, and no one knew how he felt about that. He took a liking to Gimpy, brought scraps for him to eat, and even took him home on weekends and school vacations. One day disaster struck—Gimpy was run over by a school bus. He survived, but lost the use of one of his front legs. Everyone thought it was all up for him but Jud fixed him a box near the furnace and looked after him until he recovered. Gimpy got around as well as ever on his three good legs and continued to do his job keeping the school mouse-free. It was about this time that Jud constructed a cat door in the lower part of the big main door, so that Gimpy could step out when he wished. Going home with Jud he trotted after him, mimicking Jud's uneven gait. Occasionally, in bad spots, Jud scooped him up and put him on his shoulder, where he hooked his claws into Jud's jacket, hanging on as they lurched homeward.

Gimpy's golden eyes observed Lindsey, he stretched towards her.

"I know, Gimpy, you want a chin rub." She stroked his throat. Gimpy's eyes closed; the beginning of his purr vibrated against Lindsey's fingers. This ritual completed, Lindsey continued up to the second floor. James sat on the banister at the top of the stair; she took her hand off the rail to go round him when she reached the top.

James smiled a greeting. He was there so often she was disappointed if he was not. She would go to talk to Barbara and her friends, paying little attention to their chatter, looking about to see where he might be. She noticed that the upperclassmen were often checking assignments with each other.

"James," she said one noon when she reached the top of the stair. "You are good at physics, aren't you?"

"Sometimes." His face colored slightly, but it wasn't a blush. He waited.

"I don't understand the last chapter we had."

"Be glad to help you," James said casually. Lindsey was relieved.

From then on she and James talked about physics, about calculus, about school assignments. Her mother asked why she rushed through her lunch to make such an early return to school. James was always at the top of the stairs. In their daily snatches of conversation she learned about the Furling farm.

"Six hundred acres." he told her, "counting the pastures up the mountain."

He told her about the cattle too. About how many cows they had in the herd, and how they had to be milked night and morning.

"Every single morning?" She asked. "And every night? What happens if you're not there, if you miss?"

"You can't miss," James said decisively. When you have cows you got to be right there, night and morning."

"What if you had to move, how would you do it?" she asked. 'It must be really hard."

"We don't move," he said.

"How can you be so sure you won't have to one day?" Lindsey told him about New Jersey, and how they had moved a dozen times that she could remember.

"I feel more at home in Twinbridge than I ever did before," she said. "We've been here almost two years."

She told James about living in New Jersey, and how, every morning her dad would walk up to the train station and take the train into New York to work in his office. She saw that James couldn't understand that kind of a life. Lindsey found that she was thinking about James a good deal. He was talking about the farm late in November, when he suddenly changed the subject.

"There's going to be a good movie on in Ransom on Friday night. Would you like to go?"

"To Ransom?"

Lindsey had never been to the movies in Ransom. Like everyone else in Twinbridge she walked down Main Street to Hamlin's movie house beyond the railroad station. Gas was rationed. No one drove eight miles to Ransom to go to a movie.

James understood her hesitation. "I drive my dad's truck," he said.

Lindsey remembered. James lived on a farm. Farmers had gasoline.

Her heart gave a little leap. "Why yes, James, I'd love to do that."

Chapter Two

The New Teacher

"What are you going to use for your book report this month, Lindsey?"

Miss Taylor's question from the front of the room surprised her. Lindsey was gathering together the books she wanted to take home, as the classroom slowly cleared out. Miss Taylor was at her desk.

"I haven't decided," she said.

"Make sure it stretches your mind." Miss Taylor said, and went back to her books.

Lindsey's homeroom teacher her sophomore year had been Mrs. Gately, who had taught English at the high school for as long as anyone could remember. Mrs. Gately was getting along in years, but she ignored hints about retirement. She enjoyed presiding in the classroom, having the bustle of young people around her. In the last few years, however, Mrs. Gately had what she called "tummy trouble," and had to spend considerable time away from her desk. Her students snickered and exchanged rude comments. She also became increasingly deaf, and could not always tell if answers were correct when she quizzed them on their English lessons. At the end of Lindsey's sophomore year Mrs. Gately finally consented to be retired with honors and a celebratory dinner in the White Church Social Hall. She was replaced by Miss Taylor, newly graduated from a Normal School in Massachusetts.

    Miss Taylor took a room on the other end of town with Mr. and Mrs. Banks, who had a spacious house and rented rooms to the single teachers. She walked briskly to school each day, across the lower bridge, along Main Street, and up the Church Street bridge. She wore a bright red knitted toque, a beacon that was visible from one end of Main Street to the other. She slowed her walk only later in the winter when her strong, angular figure picked its way over icy patches of sidewalk. In her classroom a new regime was gradually established. It became quieter. It also became neater. The boys learned that Miss Taylor objected to books or jackets flung on windowsills or stuffed under desks. She insisted too, that they raise their hands to ask questions, and answer intelligibly when addressed.

Lindsey thought of Miss Taylor's admonition to stretch her mind. Why did she say that to her, and not to the entire class? Did Miss Taylor think that she, Lindsey, was lazy? She pondered, walking home. Surely not. None of her teachers had ever accused Lindsey of being lazy.

"Miss Taylor told me I ought to have a book report that stretches my mind," she told her mother when she reached home.

"What did she mean by that?"

"I don't know."

Lindsey decided to visit Mrs. Cartwright, the chief and only librarian of the Twinbridge Public Library. The library had formerly housed the bank and its atmosphere was formal and strait-laced, befitting a custodian of money. Its dull green carpeting was still in good condition. The library had inherited several usable swivel chairs when the bank moved into its larger building down the street, chairs especially popular with younger readers who liked to sit in them and push themselves along the shelves in the children's section looking for appealing titles.

Mrs. Cartwright sat in her accustomed place, at her desk on a raised platform in the center of the room. From there she surveyed her clients as they entered. Her pink, plastic-rimmed spectacles sat firmly in the middle of her round face which was framed by white curls in wig-like order. Her costume, too was invariable: a white jabot under a buttoned black jacket. She took off her wet boots when she entered and put on comfortable felt slippers which rested on a cushion beneath her desk.

Years previously, Lindsey had approached this throne cautiously with her assignments. She feared this austere figure, reminiscent of a picture she had once seen of a medieval English judge. She soon found that Mrs. Cartwright, appearances to the contrary, was a friendly soul, pleased to have company, and anxious to be of use. She went to no end of trouble to satisfy her patrons, even calling up the libraries in Ransom or South Twinbridge to find books. She gave up this practice when she found there was no satisfactory way to transport them to Twinbridge. She kept the stove on the side of the room stoked; it was cozy in the library even on blustery days. She also had an electric hot-plate and could bring her kettle to the boil at a moment's notice.

"Would you like a cup of tea?" she had asked Lindsey one day while they looked for a reference book that was out of place.

Lindsey had never been offered tea. Tea belonged to her mother's generation. She was intrigued. "I'd like that," she said.

Mrs. Cartwright indicated a chair beside a small table behind her desk, a table spread with a blue striped cloth and set with two heavy white cups and saucers. She poured boiling water into the cups and pushed a container holding a tarnished silver tea ball across the table. Lindsey dipped it into her cup and took one spoonful of sugar. She would have taken more but feared it might be impolite since sugar was rationed.

Today, as she walked up the two icy steps and grasped the cold brass knob to enter the library, she was intent upon her mission. She explained to Mrs. Cartwright, "I need a book for a report. Miss Taylor said be sure and get one that would stretch my mind."

"So she doesn't want you to pick something too easy," Mrs. Cartwright said. She thought for a moment. "I suppose you've read The Yearling?"

Lindsey admitted she had not. She remembered hearing a lot about it a few years before. They agreed that Miss Taylor would approve of it. Lindsey went to the "R's" and found it quickly. Moisture had stained its green cover, and mottled the spine, buts its pages were undamaged. Mrs. Cartwright stamped her library card, and she bore it away. She began reading it that night, sitting up in bed. The dialect was not the easiest but she got used to it, and was absorbed in the story of the boy and his deer. She wept when the boy was compelled to destroy the animal that he loved. She thought about it a lot and spent more time than usual writing her report.

She had it ready to hand it in on the day it was due in English class. Miss Taylor did not say, "Hand the book reports down front, please," as Mrs. Gately had always done. Instead she said, "Why don't we read our reports to the class? You can begin, Lindsey."

Her square face tipped in Lindsey's direction, her eyes large behind her glasses. Lindsey always felt like a bug under a microscope with Miss Taylor. She stumbled at first in the reading, but steadied herself as she went along. When she finished, Miss Taylor rapped the desk. "Very good, Lindsey. You spent your time well."

Lindsey tried to look off-hand and humble, but she could not help feeling pleased.

I'll have to tell Mrs. Cartwright.

Chapter Three

Trip to Ransom

Lindsey made sure to be ready the night James came to pick her up. He peeled off his cap as she opened the door for him. His hair stood on end around his smooth face when he entered the warm room, his cheeks red from the cold.

Lindsey put him to sit opposite her parents in the living room while she fetched her coat. She eavesdropped on their brief exchange.

"Do you think we'll be having snow tonight?" her father said.

"It's starting already," James said. He squirmed in his chair, facing her dad. "They'll have the plows out by morning."

"We're going to the movies in Ransom," Lindsey said as she came to James' rescue. Of course she had already told them; they knew where she was going. She twisted her scarf high about her neck, and pulled on her mittens, following James out.

It was cold in the cabin of James' old truck, cold enough for their breaths to make billowy clouds before the heater warmed up. The snow swirled in feathery flakes, traces already showing along the sides of the flat, curving road to Ransom. It was not yet sticking to the paving; their headlights traced a black-bottomed path into the darkness. Occasionally a car came from the opposite direction, its flaring white lights blinding them momentarily as it passed. James was silent, his gloved hands on the wheel, his attention on the road. She felt cocooned in the rattling truck, glancing sideways at his profile, wanting to talk, deterred by his silence.

Ransom was a more important town than Twinbridge. It boasted a large common, edged with store fronts; the movie theater was on one side. They arrived early. She stood beside James under the shelter of the small marque while James bought their tickets. They entered, then, into the narrow lobby where others already stood about, waiting for the theater doors to open. The white-washed walls were decorated with autographed pictures of movie stars, along with several posters of upcoming attractions. Lindsey was relieved to find there was no one she knew from Twinbridge—it was always possible, even though unlikely. She did not have to make awkward talk, or fear that gossip would whisper its way around town that Lindsey had been on a date with James Furling in Ransom.

The doors opened promptly. She and James were among the first to enter the dimly lit theater. They turned into the last row but one, and took the seats furthest from the aisle. James helped Lindsey out of her coat; she settled it around her shoulders. Gradually the theater filled. Since it was a Friday night couples like themselves sought quiet corners. Groups of girls called to each other across the rows, switching their places, settling down. The overhead lights flicked on and off, and then went out; latecomers groped their way to seats in the dark. They heard the footsteps of the projectionist in the balcony above; he entered the booth and pulled the door shut behind him. The chatter of the audience quieted. In a few minutes the projector whirred as it started up; a mote-filled beam of light appeared and lit up the large rectangular screen on the stage. The black-and-white Pathé newsreel began. The familiar, soothing voice of the announcer accompanied the grainy pictures flickering over the now-commonplace scenes of death and destruction. American airmen waved as they climbed into their bombers to take off from English airfields and lay waste more German cities; landing craft lay off unnamed Pacific islands. The audience sat in passive silence as the newsreel summed up the war.

The technicolor image of the MGM lion filled the screen. He turned his great head; two guttural roars signaled the start of the main attraction, the musical "Pin-Up Girl," starring Betty Grable. Its slender plot unfolded. Lindsey rested her hand on the thin padded arm between herself and James. He leaned closer; his shoulder pressed against hers. She sat stiffly, distracted by his nearness. Tentatively, his hand closed over hers. She moved her hand enough to curl her fingers over his. The theater's warm darkness wrapped around them as they sat bound together watching the screen's display of moving color

    The movie over, they exited the theater into still-falling snow. The frosty air filled their lungs, doubly cold after the stuffy warmth of the theater. As James started the truck, they kept up an exchange about the movie they had seen. She slid across the slippery cold of the leather seat to sit closer to him, and tucked her coat around her legs.

"Take a while to warm up the truck again," he said. "Next time I'll bring you a blanket."

Lindsey savoring the words 'next time' did not feel the cold, now that she was sitting close to James.

The snow, falling rapidly, masked the blacktop, but their trip home was swift. The living room lights shone at the windows of Lindsey's house; her parents sometimes stayed up to listen to the late news.

"Would you like to come in?"

Lindsey knew she ought to ask, and was relieved when he declined. She admitted to herself that she did not want to end the evening making awkward conversation with her parents. Lindsey tried not to be embarrassed by them, she knew she should be loyal, but it was no use. Everyone must notice how different they were if she noticed it herself. Her parents did not fit in. They even looked different. Her father wore an overcoat instead of a jacket, and a fedora hat with a brim instead of a cap. When he walked out with her mother he held her arm even if the streets were not slippery. Instead of doing their shopping on Saturday nights, like everyone else, her parents shopped on a weekday afternoon. Her dad came home from the garage early, and they walked to Main Street together. They took their ration books to Blossom's Butcher Store, and bought the hamburger for the week. Then they went on to Hedley's to buy their groceries. If it was more than one bag Lindsey stopped by to pick up the second one after school. Her parents knew everyone in town, but they didn't have any friends. It had been the same way in all the other places they had lived in since they left New Jersey. They were from New York and the Jersey suburbs, and had nothing in common with their neighbors in these small New England towns.

James' father got up at dawn and milked cows. Her father walked up over the bridge at eight o'clock and sat at a desk looking at account books all day. Lindsey's mother had never been on a farm in her life, and Mrs. Furling had probably never been off one.

They are outsiders. They don't fit in.

Lindsey was sorry, because she herself was not an outsider. She felt at home. She fit in.

Chapter Four

Saturday Night

On Saturday night Lindsey cleared the dinner table and helped her mother with the dishes, lingering in the kitchen after she had hung up the dish towel.

"The girls are getting together to go downtown," she said. "Do you need anything?"

The shops stayed open late on Saturday evenings, it was their busiest time. Once the week's work on the farms ended, and the chores were done, families came to town to take care of their shopping. The men bought sacks of feed at the mill while their wives ran their own errands. Carrying small children and trailed by older ones, women gathered in groups up and down Main Street to exchange the news.

Lindsey thought a lot about what she would wear that night. She had a scarf her aunt had sent her last year that was too good to wear to school, but it matched her coat. She looked at her reflection in the mirror over the sink while she adjusted the metal band of her fuzzy blue earmuffs. She settled the warm circlets directly over her ears.

"All dressed up, you are, tonight," her mother said, watching her. "You're just going with the girls?"

"Yes, Mom."

"Well, see you get back about ten."

Lindsey met Barbara and her other friends in front of the telephone company. They crossed the foot of the bridge to stroll up Main Street toward the movie theater. As they passed the mill, she saw a flash of red up ahead: Miss Taylor's knitted hat. Miss Taylor stood in front of Blossom's Butcher Shop, her trim body slightly tipped toward her taller companion. Lindsey recognized James' father, his pepper and salt hair brushed back and uncovered. They appeared to be having a discussion. He listened attentively as Miss Taylor spoke, her elbows turned out, her hands in motion.

If Mr. Furling is here, James is, too.

Lindsey and her friends continued on, crossing the street in front of the library, and returning past the post office and the hotel. She watched for James, fearing she had missed him in the crowd. The girls had started on their second tour up Main Street when Barbara elbowed her sharply.

"Lindsey, look!" she said, giggling. "There he is!"

Lindsey caught sight of his blue jacket. He was in front of the train station, leaning against the brass railing that edged the sidewalk. She was sure he was looking for her. Maybe he had come up from the pool room behind the station. She had heard the boys went there to sneak a beer on Saturday nights.

James straightened and stepped forward to fall into step with her as she drew alongside. Barbara and the girls crossed the street to mingle with other friends. James moved to her left to walk on the curb, where it was slushy with half-melted ice. He tucked his hand under her elbow.

"I thought I'd never get through with the milking tonight," James looked down at her. His smile made her catch her breath.

"I was beginning to think you weren't going to be here." She pressed his hand against her side.

"Let's see if we can get us a booth at Hedley's," he said.

There was a crowd on the steps there; women going in and out and standing at the counter, buying what they needed to add to the canned goods they had put up in the fall. Chuck Hedley and his hired man, Clyde, moved back and forth behind the counter to pull boxes and cans down from the shelves, efficiently wrapping them in bundles, binding them with twine. Lindsey and James made their way by the counter and passed through the open archway that led to the back room.

A light bulb with a dark metal shade hung high above a pool table in the center of the room, its light shining through a pall of cigarette smoke. The chalk-tipped cues shot across the smooth green baize, striking the balls, propelling them swiftly into the side pockets. The players strode around the table, intent on their game. Lindsey and James threaded their way through the on-lookers to the booths on the back wall.

Before the war, the Hedleys had planned to open a lunch counter. Chuck's father-in-law, a carpenter, had built six booths along the wall in the back room. Chuck gave up on the idea when the war started and the young people left for the army or the defense plants. The pool table in the middle of the room remained, as did the six booths which operated on a self-serve basis. Lindsey and James were lucky to find the corner booth free on a Saturday night. He brought their Cokes from the ice chest and picked up two glasses from the counter. They squeezed in behind the scarred wooden table; Lindsey was conscious of James' thigh pressed against hers. She felt sheltered in the darkened booth, happy that no one took any notice of her.

"James," Lindsey said, "can I ask you a question?"

"Why sure," he said. "What do you want to know?"

"There are lots of people named James, but no one is ever called that. They're all called Jimmy. Why are you called James?"

He laughed. "You've got the answer right there," he said. "Our family was full of Jameses. My grandfather was James, and he was named for his dad, so my great-grandfather, he was James too. My dad, and half of his cousins were named James, and half of my cousins too, and they were all called Jimmy. Ma called me James just to keep it straight who they were talking about."

"I like you being called James. It makes you sound important, dignified."

"That's something I'm never going to be," he said. "Farmers are lots of things, but dignified isn't one of them."

"And you want to be a farmer?"

"For sure. We got a patch of good land there by the river, couldn't ask for better, and pastures up on the mountain for the cows."

"So many people now work in town, like in the post office, and take care of their farms part-time. You wouldn't want to do that?"

He shook his head decisively. "They're only doing that because times are hard, and they're cash-hungry. What happens is they got to get hired men to do the work they don't have time to do, and their farms get run down because those fellas do things the easiest way, not the best way. They don't care."

He shook his head again. "Not for me. I might have me a hired hand or two – probably will someday – but I'll be working right beside 'em, and know what they are up to." He took a long swig of his Coke. "But we were talking about names. I never heard of anybody named Lindsey. Where did that come from?"

"My mother's name," Lindsey explained. "She doesn't have any brothers, so there aren't going to be any more Lindseys. Kids made fun of me for having a last name for a first name, but I got used to it, now I don't care."

"Kids pick on other kids, if it wasn't for your name it would be something else." James said. "They picked on me in grade school because I was little and scrawny. But then I grew some, and they quit."

"Can't imagine you little and scrawny, James" she said, looking up at him.

"Been a while since anybody messed with me,"

Later, when he walked her home, they stood in the shadow of the linden tree in front of her house, their faces pale blurs in the frosty darkness. His light beard scraped her cheek and, awkwardly, their lips met; she closed her eyes. She rested her mittened hand on his shoulder, his hand slipped around her waist. His cold nose bumped against hers; she opened her eyes and saw that his were closed. Hastily she stepped back.

"I better go in."

"See you Monday," he said, as she opened the porch door. He stayed there in the shadows while she pulled the door shut.

In the living room, her mother was on the couch and her dad sat in his chair beside her with the Saturday Evening Post in his lap. Lindsey knew he had been reading a story aloud while her mother crocheted.

"Did you have a good time?" her mother asked.

"Oh, yes, it was fun seeing everyone." Lindsey walked through to hang her coat. She looked in the mirror over the sink in the kitchen to check that her hair was in place before she joined them.

Chapter Five

The New York Times

Lindsey's dad had a standing order at Mrs. Martin's drug store for the Sunday New York Times. It was days late by the time he received it, but he said it was the only way to get any real news.

"We hear the news every night on the radio," Lindsey said. "Aren't you reading it again in the newspaper?"

Apparently he was not. He settled himself in the chair beside the couch and held the paper open before him like a tent. Lindsey and her mother never asked him to do anything while he read The Times. He went through it slowly, page by page, first the war news, then the financial pages. The latter demanded his special attention; he studied them carefully to see how the stock market was doing. When he had finished he gave Lindsey and her mother a short summary of what he had learned, concluding with his opinion of Mr. Roosevelt, never complimentary.

In the paper's entertainment section, which her father laid aside, Lindsey read about new movies, and the movie stars. Plays and musicals opening on Broadway were also reviewed. Lindsey got in the habit of reading about them, too. She learned the names of the actors and actresses and knew who was starring in each one. She dreamed of the day she would order tickets to a great performance. She even gave thought to which section of the theater; she knew it was best to be in the orchestra, she even checked the price of orchestra seats.

*   *   *   *   *

"There's a new musical, Oklahoma!" Lindsey said to Barbara as they watched for enemy planes. "It's a smash hit."

It had been on a Saturday in August. She and Barbara had volunteered for duty in the hut during the summer. First they had had to convince their parents that they would come to no harm alone up there.

"It's only a third of a mile up from the Anderson's farmhouse," Lindsey pointed out. "We walk there all the time in the summer: nothing happens to us."

The path through the Anderson's farm became steep as it curved up to the hut. It was slippery and hard walking during the spring mud season. In the winter the men, freed from the summer chores, had to do heavy shoveling to keep the path open.

The second time she and Barbara were on duty they spotted a plane, far to the west, silent, moving slowly. Barbara called the Army Filter Center on the special phone while Lindsey wrote the information in the log. Since that exciting day, they had been to the hut a number of times but had seen nothing more. They whiled away the time gossiping. Lindsey brought along The Times entertainment section and read Barbara bits from it. On that particular afternoon, to get Barbara's attention, she repeated, "A new musical, Oklahoma!"

"Where?"

"On Broadway, of course."

"That's in New York. We aren't going to see it here."

"New York's not so far."

"Farther than we'll ever get." Barbara held the binoculars to her eyes, to sweep the horizon. She saw only pale sky, and the fringe of evergreens rimming the mountains from west to east. The hut, built to the specifications set forth by the Aircraft Warning Service, maximized the broad view.

Lindsey stopped reading.

"I've got a great idea, let's go to New York."

"Lindsey, what are you talking about?"

"I mean to go to school. College."

Barbara looked at Lindsey, frowning.

"Why would we do that? When we can go to the university in Burlington, right here in state?"

"If we went to school in New York we could see the plays on Broadway. We could visit Times Square and the Statue of Liberty and see all those wonderful places we've read about."

"My folks would never let me," Barbara said.

They discussed it, off and on, for the next hour, until Grant Sterling came up the path to take the next shift.

Mr. Sterling was a cousin of Barbara's father; his farm adjoined the Anderson's. He was a tall man, his overalls, patched on both knees, were too short. He signed his name in precise, large letters into the log, with the exact time.

Lindsey was quiet as they walked down the hill, her thoughts still on New York. She knew Barbara was right about how her parents would feel about her going there. Barbara's father was born and brought up on a farm in Twinbridge; her mother came from Ransom. They would see no point in Barbara going to New York to go to school.

Her own parents might object at first to the idea of her going so far away. She was sure she could persuade them. They were New Yorkers, they had grown up in the city. How could they deny her, having seen it all themselves?

Now that the snow had come she and Barbara were no longer going to the hut on the mountain to watch for enemy planes. She continued to read about shows on Broadway in the New York Times, and to dream of seeing "Oklahoma!"

What about James?

She sighed. She knew that, like Barbara, he would not be interested in leaving his farm in Twinbridge to go to New York, not even to see "Oklahoma!"

Chapter Six

The Christmas Locket

The war dragged on. James and seven of his classmates—all the boys in the senior class—signed their draft papers and were deferred from service until graduation. In December, Bing Crosby's voice was on every radio station singing "White Christmas," and "I'll be Home for Christmas." Everyone listened to the evening news to learn the progress of the war. In 1943, none of the men or women in the service came home for Christmas. They were too far away, overseas in England waiting for the invasion everyone knew was coming, or on ships in the Pacific, fighting from island to island. Their families waited for letters that came seldom and told nothing.

Lindsey walked home from school one grey afternoon the week before Christmas and was surprised to see James waiting at the foot of the bridge. Usually, he was gone before she gathered her books together. He had to get home to help his dad. The longer it took them to start chores, she knew, the longer it took to finish the evening milking.

He smiled down at her as she came up to him. His ears, below his cap, were as red from the cold as his cheeks.

"I've got something for you." He fumbled in his jacket pocket. "For Christmas. I'm sorry it isn't wrapped." He held out a crumpled brown bag, barely visible in his bulky glove.

"Oh, James, I haven't even thought about Christmas." She put out her hand and he placed it in her palm. "Should I open it now or wait till I get home?"

He paused, considering.

"Open it Christmas morning."

There was no one else on the bridge. He folded her fingers over the package, gave her a quick kiss on the cheek, and was gone.

Lindsey showed the package to her parents; they teased her about it.

"You'll have it opened before Christmas," her mother said.

But on Christmas Eve she placed it on her bedside table. In the half-light of early morning she brought it under the covers and pulled away the brown paper to uncover a blue velvet jewelry box. She pressed its tiny latch to make it spring open. Inside was a gold locket on a chain. She traced its flower motif with her little finger, and saw how the locket was designed to hold two photographs.

"You like the box as much as you do the locket," her mother remarked later.

It was true. Lindsey loved to rub her fingers gently on the nubby velvet, to press the tiny lever that popped it open. Upstairs in the evenings under the bedcovers in her chilly room, she took the little box from her dresser drawer, lifting the locket from its creased nest of white taffeta with great care to avoid entangling its fine chain. Under the light of her table lamp, she moved her thumb across its surface to add to its shine, and slid her nail under the indentation that allowed it to open. After a few minutes she replaced it as carefully, adjusting the chain to make the perfect "V" that held it in place.

Lindsey wore the locket every day underneath her sweater where it could not be seen. She wore it openly only on those evenings that she and James went to the movies.

Chapter Seven

The Davis Place

"Would you go to the post office, Lindsey?" her mother asked one Friday afternoon in early January. "I'm waiting for a letter."

Lindsey's aunt in Jersey, her mother's sister Ruth wasn't well; her mother was anxious to hear from her.

The mail train pulled into the station at five o'clock. Lindsey, walking from home, heard its mournful call as it rounded the curve below the lower bridge. Sam, who worked in the post office, crossed Main Street when the train approached, in time to pick up the sack of mail that would be tossed down as the train paused in the station. Lindsey saw Sam re-enter the back door of the post office as she walked up the steps to the front entrance. People had already begun to gather. Men, some women too, crowded into the poorly lit ante-room, bundled in their coats, silent, waiting for the mail to be distributed. Sam and Greg, in the back room, stuffed letters into the glass-fronted boxes of the dividing wall. No one moved until the muffled call came, "mail's all up," then pushed forward to open their boxes, their boots shuffling on the worn floorboards. There was little mail that evening. Most came away empty handed, as did Lindsey. With the others, she headed out into the dark for home. She was on the top step when she saw James' truck pulling to the curb.

"Lindsey, wait, I'll drive you home," he called. Her heart lurched in her chest, seeing him, happy at the unexpected meeting.

She climbed into the truck and James swung it around in the train station lot.

"I got to drive Ma to her sister's tomorrow, won't get back till late," he said. "How about if I pick you up after lunch Sunday? We can drive around and I can show you the farm."

Despite the disheartening news she brought to her mother, Lindsey felt a warm glow, thinking of the time that she would spend with James.

Main Street was deserted on Sunday, bare of all its Saturday night activity. Two cars passed, splattering a sprinkle of ice onto the sidewalk. The cold sun glittered on the windshield as James twisted the wheel to turn right off the main road immediately after the lower bridge. They bumped along a narrow gravel road for a quarter of a mile, James pointing out the Furling barn on the right, as they passed it, the gate of the barnyard propped open off the road. He parked the truck a few feet further on, in front of the house. It was large, painted a tired white, the shutters and the banister on the three steps leading to the wide porch were black. The porch came to an end on the right; on the left it cornered the house. James pushed open the resisting door; a blast of warm air met them as they entered the kitchen.

"James, I'm so glad you got here," Mrs. Furling said, after she had greeted Lindsey. "I've got some food to send up to the Davises and Dad is busy in the barn. You can run it up in the truck, keep it warm"

"Someone sick?" asked James. ""

"Mr. Davis fell last night, hurt his leg. And you know she hasn't been doing well for a while."

Mrs. Furling, as she chattered on, prepared kettles of food, and wrapped baked goods.

"Sure, Ma," James said. "Lindsey and I will take it. She can see the view from up there."

Together, they bundled the kettles into the cab of the truck, on the seat between them.

"The Davis farm borders ours on the top of the hill," James explained. He backed the truck away from the porch and followed the meandering road up the hill behind the house. "From way back, in my grandfather's time. Maybe not for much longer."

"Why not?" Lindsey asked.

"Mr. Davis is getting too old to farm," James said. "There's a couple of daughters, already married and moved away, neither of 'em is interested in keeping the farm going."

They reached the top of the hill, and James pointed out landmarks that showed where the Furling pastures ended and the Davis fields began. In the distance she glimpsed the Davis house, on the right. It disappeared as they followed the curving road, and came into view again.

"Oh, what a nice house," Lindsey said. It fit so snugly into its place, in its cleft of the curve, beckoning, inviting. It was well-kept, the paved walkway led neatly from the parking area at the side, to the kitchen entrance, sheltered by its small porch a step above the walk. The walkway continued around the corner of a larger section of the house, to the front door, similarly covered by a larger portico. There was a barn, smaller than the Furling barn, to the rear of the house.

"It looks like a happy house," she said to James.

He looked down at her. For some reason her remark seemed to annoy him. "Houses aren't happy or unhappy," he said. "They just are."

"Some look like they are easier to be happy in." She had carried the conversation further than she intended.

"Let's get this food in while it's hot."

They rapped at the kitchen door, and in a moment it was pulled open by a smiling Mrs. Davis. She was small, so small that Lindsey thought for a moment it was a child gesturing them to enter, but saw immediately the fluff of gray hair and the starting stoop of age. Mrs. Davis clapped her hands when she saw the foodstuffs they unloaded on the kitchen table.

"Your Ma is so kind, James," she said. "She's always the first one at the door when you need help. Lindsey, I've seen you enough in town so I feel like I know you." She moved about, arranging some items on the back of the stove, putting others away. Lindsey, seeing they would stay for a few minutes, slipped out of her jacket, and looked about the large kitchen. The two windows looked to the southwest; the mid-afternoon sun filled the room. On one side, faced to the sun, was a couch covered in brown corduroy, with several yellow cushions at either end.

Mr. Davis sat in a large chair at one end of the couch, his legs extended on an ottoman and covered with an afghan knit in bright stripes. James went to him to shake his hand. Mrs. Davis introduced Lindsey. Lindsey, who noticed that his face was drawn, understood why James had said, "He's getting too old to farm."

"Didn't need this," he said to James. "Too much to do to have a leg give out on you."

"If it's got to happen, the winter's the best time," James told him. "You'll be fit when it's time to do the spring planting."

They took their leave shortly, bearing away with them Mrs. Davis' hearty thanks to James' mother. The truck was chilly, and now, without the food on the seat, she sat close to James.

"He doesn't look so good," James observed, and she agreed.

"What will happen to them, James?"

"He'll manage to hang on for a few years more. But with no one to take the farm over he's going to have to sell out." James shifted gears as they came to the top of the hill. He paused, looking to either side.

"When he's ready to sell, I plan to buy."

"James!" she said. "Seriously?"

"Seriously." He laughed. "I'm always thinking about it. You can make a great farm out of the Davis place."

"And the house, James. It's special." She reminded herself that for James it was the land that was special, not the house.

"Let's stop home for a hot toddy," James said. "Then I'll drive you home."

They arrived at the Furlings' at the same time Mr. Furling came in from the barn. The cows were already out in the barnyard; Lindsey knew that within the hour James and his father would need to start the milking. Lindsey regretted now that she had agreed to the hot toddy. She would have preferred to make some excuse about a promise to her mother and to walk along the road toward home. Her thoughts hummed in her mind; she heard James' quick voice saying "When he has to sell, I plan to buy."

Mr. Furling discussed some farm problem with James. Uneasily she watched them across the kitchen. He was tall, broad-shouldered, except for his graying hair still youthful looking. James was a copy of him. They stood in the same way, leaning slightly backward. It was their expressions that marked the difference in them. James face was open, reflective of his moods. It was what she found appealing about him. His father's was a curtain, hiding his thoughts.

Why does he make me uneasy?

James drove her home. Lindsey put Mr. Furling out of her mind, and lingered over thoughts of what life would be like as a farmer's wife.

Chapter Eight

Mrs. Cartwright's Library

On this day, visiting the library, Lindsey brought a bag of cookies from her mother. She and Mrs. Cartwright shared them while the librarian looked over her current requests.

"Dickens, *A Tale of Two Cities*," Mrs. Cartwright said. "So different from the rest of Dickens. The very one I don't have, unfortunately."

"I can wait and get it in the school library," Lindsey said, helping herself to several spoons of sugar. "They don't have *The Pickwick Papers,* though."

"I always thought that a bit of a bore," Mrs. Cartwright reached for the kettle to freshen up their cups of tea, took another cookie, and settled back. "So what is this about you and James Furling? And don't ask me what I mean. I have eyes in my head."

Lindsey set her cup down onto the damp saucer. She felt the color in her cheeks. "We go to the movies," was all she could think of to say.

"He's a reliable boy," Mrs. Cartwright said. Lindsey heard the tick-tocking of the clock on the wall behind the desk marking time with her heart. "What are his plans for the future?"

"The same as all the boys," Lindsey said. "He'll get called up as soon as he graduates."

"I meant after that. When this war is over and they all come back."

"I've never thought about that. It's so many years away."

"It will come. You best think about it now. Are you sure you want to be a farmer's wife?"

Why is she asking me? My parents don't, why should she?

Lindsey felt a knot of resentment in the pit of her stomach. She did not want to have this conversation, but didn't quite know how to cut it off.

"Not any of my business, you are thinking," Mrs. Cartwright reached behind her to pick up a sock and a darner from the corner of her desk. "You're right. I've got a nerve."

The front door cracked open and a cold blast of air entered as an over-coated figure stamped his galoshes in the doorway. It was Mr. Cartwright. Quick as a cat, Mrs. Cartwright jumped to her feet and was at the door.

"Come in, come in, don't hold the door open." She grasped her husband's arm and pulled him into the room, pushing the door shut behind him. His glasses fogged up in the heated room; he stood sightless, motionless. Once the lenses cleared his bloodshot eyes showed glazed and unknowing.

Lindsey stood up. "I better go."

Mrs. Cartwright, Lindsey knew, had to take care of her husband. She would put him to sit on the bench back of the bookcases until she closed the library, and would lead him home to their little house on Water Street to spoon hot soup into him, and get him to bed. He would be better by tomorrow.

Lindsey said goodbye to Mrs. Cartwright and let herself out to walk home in the thickening dusk.

"How is Mrs. Cartwright?" In the kitchen her mother glanced up from the codfish cakes she was frying for supper.

"Mr. Cartwright came in while I was there. He was having one of his spells."

"Poor woman," her mother rapped the spatula sharply on the edge of the frying pan. "She didn't realize when she married him that she was going to spend her life sobering him up."

Lindsey, half out of her coat, considered. "But Mom, nobody knows, do they? When you and Dad got married he was a broker on Wall Street, with his own business and you lived in New Jersey. You didn't know you were going to wind up here in Vermont."

Her mother waited a minute before answering, turning over the codfish cakes at the precise moment that they were brown and crusty on the bottom, and heated through.

"Hard times happen," she said. "When they do there's nothing to do except get through them. It's when you have choices that you have to take care."

Lindsey heard her father coming in the front door, scraping his feet on the mat.

"Time to eat," her mother said. She transferred the codfish cakes to a platter and handed it to

Lindsey, bringing along a bowl of cole slaw to the dining room table.

They sat, the three of them, mostly silent as her mother passed the food and they ate. They wanted to be finished by the time the evening news came on.

Chapter Nine

The Telephone Company

It was Mrs. Cartwright, a few weeks later, who told Lindsey about the job in the telephone company. "Go ask them," she said. "They need a spare operator to work nights."

"But I've never done anything like that,"

"None of 'em had before they started," said Mrs. Cartwright. "Won't hurt to ask. You said you wanted to earn money."

Lindsey delayed for three more days, but one afternoon she forced herself to go. She mounted the three stairs of the prim stucco building at the foot of the bridge and pushed open the door into the entrance hall. To her right, beyond a railing, two ladies wearing headphones and holding cables perched on high stools in front of a telephone board. To her left was an office where, behind a counter, a small, sharp-faced lady sat typing rapidly. Miss Primble nodded to Lindsey, mouthing, "one minute," as she continued typing. Lindsey waited until she ripped the completed paper from her typewriter.

"Mrs. Cartwright told me you were looking for someone to be a night operator. She said I should come and see you."

"I've been expecting you," Miss Primble said.

Lindsey instantly felt guilt about the three-day delay.

"A junior in high school, are you? Where do you live?"

Lindsey pointed across the street, and told Miss Primble she was indeed a junior. Miss Primble's brisk manner softened.

"Lucy Cartwright told me you were a sensible girl," she said. "We can try you out, and you can see how you like it. At first you'd work in the daytime with one of the other operators. Eventually you'd be on at night by yourself. There's a cot back there where you can stretch out after it quiets down, and you put the night bell on. I suppose you'd like to know what you'd get paid?"

Lindsey had hoped Miss Primble would bring it up.

"Mom, they will pay me thirty-five cents an hour," Lindsey told her mother. "Thirty-five cents! She said come on Saturday morning, and one of the operators will start training me."

Lindsey hurried up the stairs at school the next day looking for James.

"James, guess what? I've got a job. I'm going to be a telephone operator. And the pay is thirty-five cents an hour!"

James laughed, looking down at her. "Thirty-five an hour! What are you going to do with all that money?"

"I'll save it," she said. "All of it. And then I will spend it all at once for something wonderful."

Saturday one of the seasoned operators, it was Carrie Spencer, initiated Lindsey into the mysteries of the telephone boards.

"When someone calls in, it buzzes and their flap falls open on the board. You plug a jack into that flap from one of the pairs at the base of the board and ask what number they want. Then you plug the second jack of the pair into the flap of the number they've asked for and the two of them are connected. Simple as that."

"I'll never get it straight," she said, near tears, to her mother that afternoon. "You can't imagine how awful it is when it gets busy."

"It will get easier. Nothing's as hard as it looks."

It was true, Lindsey decided some weeks later. She began to feel more comfortable taking her place in the second operator's chair. She was able to hold her own in the bursts of activity signaled by the buzzing of the flaps falling open in quick succession.

Lindsey took her first pay check to the bank on Main Street,

"Are you going to want to write checks on it?" Mr. Benning asked her.

"No," Lindsey said. "I want to save it." She received a passbook for a savings account and watched as Mr. Benning entered her first deposit. In her room that night, she took it out and noted the entry at the top of the page. She dreamed of ways to spend the money she saved. She heard James saying "When he has to sell, I plan to buy."

"Jane Fiske called in sick," Miss Primble said one Saturday morning. "Can you work tonight? Laura Simmons is on until nine, she can get you started."

"It's going to be fine," Mrs. Simmons said, putting on her wraps. "It gets real quiet by eleven. Just be sure the night bell is on when you go to stretch out."

"I remembered," she told James. "It was busy for an hour and then got quiet, like she said."

"One night I'll call you. My folks are dead asleep by ten."

It was the following week, close to eleven, when she heard the small complaining buzz of the Furling flap, and saw it fall. She plugged in the jack, and slid the lever back to open the line.

"Can I help you? she said, in her operator voice. It might not be James.

"It's me," he said softly into her ear. Her heart leaped.

"How are you, James?"

"I'd be better if I was right there with you."

Lindsey worked overnight at the telephone company whenever they had need of her. When Mrs. Simmons' daughter in Burlington had a baby Lindsey took her overnight shift for a week.

Lindsey found ways to let James know when she was on over-night duty at the phone company. She looked for the Furling flap to fall, with its faint buzz. Her heart beat faster at the sound of James' voice in her ear, speaking of times to come. In her bed at night she watched the entries in her passbook increase.

Chapter Ten

James' Graduation

Lindsey walked with James up and down Main Street on Saturday evenings as the snow and ice of winter gave way to the muddy slush of early April, and then to dry remnants that were swept away by May.

She reveled in the retreat of the cold. A light jacket replaced her heavy coat, and by late May, she promenaded in short-sleeved blouses. The sun's increasing warmth on her bare arms made her feel free, unencumbered. She could almost forget that each passing day was one day closer to James' graduation in mid-June, and the day that he would go off to war.

She determined to put it out of her mind. But on June 6th, a somber voice on the radio announced the landings of allied forces in France, the invasion so long anticipated. In the week that followed, James and two of his classmates received orders to report to Camp Blanding in Florida, days after their graduation.

She wanted to be with James during the days remaining, but he had little time.

I been showing Randy everything he has to do about the herd," he said to Lindsey at the top of the stairs. Randy was the high school boy who would help Mr. Furling after James left. "There's a lot he doesn't know. I can see we should have started sooner."

Lindsey wore her locket openly now. Barbara noticed.

"When did you get that?" she said, holding it out on its chain, as they stood with their friends in the hall after lunch.

James himself didn't seem to notice. He spoke only about the farm, and how his dad was going to manage without him.

*   *   *   *   *

The rows of folding chairs were already set up in the Town Hall when Lindsey's junior class went the day before graduation to rehearse their part in the program. Miss Taylor had composed a special musical tribute for the Class of '44. Lindsey was in the chorus. Miss Taylor directed, with vigor from below the stage, and Mrs. Harbin accompanied them, not well, on the piano. They had rehearsed previously, but this was their first run-through on the stage. Miss Taylor kept them at it until it went smoothly.

Lindsey's parents came to the graduation to see her performance. Her father almost backed out at the last minute. He felt uneasy about missing the evening news at this crucial time in the war; he religiously followed the broadcasts every night. Her mother persuaded him.

"We'll catch up with the war on the late news," she said. "You don't get to hear Lindsey sing very often."

Lindsey went early to sit with her class.

"Mom, make Dad come before the last minute, it will be crowded," she said before she left.

In spite of her admonitions, it was near starting time when they came in. They found places toward the front, in the first five or six rows. They sat next to the Blossoms; Lindsey imagined Clyde had to rush to finish at the butcher shop. The Shaws and the Prestons sat in the next row back, chatting together. Mr. Blossom twisted around to say something to them, laughing loudly at their reply. Her parents talked quietly to each other. They always acted as if they were by themselves, Lindsey thought, even when they were part of a crowd.

The program began, and the musical tribute was soon completed. The chorus members settled themselves again in the audience. Lindsey watched James receive his diploma. He crossed the stage confidently when his name was called, pausing in front of the principal to have his hand shaken as he accepted his rolled-up scroll.

Lindsey had no opportunity to congratulate him. He left the Hall with his class; she crossed the street to the telephone company to work the night shift. He called as he always did, but she could not take the usual pleasure in hearing his voice. The shadow of his coming departure lay between them.

Chapter Eleven

Off to War

James and the boys from his class reporting to Camp Blanding left three days later on the nine o'clock evening train. It was a fine night, full of stars as the day faded. The station lamps along the platform brightened in the darkness, shining on clustered families. Younger siblings hovered at the edges, sensing the gravity of seeing their brothers off to war.

Lindsey's father argued about going to the station. "No one's asked us," he said.

"It's not an asking thing," her mother told him. "Everyone just goes. Lindsey wants to go and she won't go alone."

Lindsey had not planned to go to the train. She had said goodbye to James in the truck that afternoon. For a few sweet minutes they pulled off on a quiet patch of the Ransom road. They kissed urgently and exchanged repeated promises to write. She wanted to savor those memories; she feared that seeing him at the train station would spoil them. In the end, she was not able to stay away. Her mother was wrong. She would have gone alone, but she was grateful they were with her. She stood behind them, away from the light, where she could see but might not be seen.

In ordinary times, the southbound train paused at the dark station, letting down the steps to one car, puffing clouds of steam, making agonized noises, impatient to get away, while a trainman swung down to assist those boarding. Tonight, Mr. Sanders, the stationmaster, opened the stationhouse, though everyone chose to wait outside on the platform.

James stood between his parents, leaning slightly toward either one as they spoke to him. Lindsey noticed for the first time that he was now taller than his father. His mother looked up first to one, then to the other. As his friends passed by, James nodded and saluted them. He continued his conversation while his eyes roved over the now-crowded platform.

He's looking for me.

The train hooted in the distance, as it approached the town from Ransom. She wanted to run to him, to throw her arms around his neck, to make a show of how she felt. The rumble grew to a roar as the train reached the underpass at the first bridge, passed behind the mill and drew into the station, obliterating conversation. James bent to kiss his mother's cheek and he and his father embraced awkwardly, clapping each other's shoulders. He turned toward the train, moving towards the open car. In another moment, he was lost to her sight as families and bystanders surged towards the tracks as the train came to a full stop. The steps were let loose from the open car to clatter down. The farewells were soon over. James was the first to climb aboard; he turned to wave, seeing her, she knew, in the crowd. The others followed, the trainman threw their bags up to them and pulled himself up. The train belched steam in quickening clouds and pulled slowly away.

Mr. Sanders extinguished the station lights and locked the empty station. The family groups moved toward the street. Lindsey and her parents followed on the heels of the Furlings as they crossed the lot.

Someone should say something.

The two families reached Main Street in silence and went their opposite ways. "They aren't very friendly, those people," her dad said to her mother.

"They just don't quite know what to say." Her mother took his arm as they walked along. Lindsey trailed after them. She didn't know what to say either.

Chapter Twelve

Lindsey's Letter

Ten days later Lindsey took the crumpled envelope from their post box. Her heart beat faster seeing James' uneven handwriting crossing the white envelope. It was a true letter, not the thin blue V-mails that came from overseas. She tucked it into the book she had checked out of the library and took it up to her room, warm now under the eaves. She opened it with care and smoothed out the pages.

"Dear Lindsey," James wrote in the first part of his letter, telling her about the training, about how different it was in Florida, and how he missed the farm. Then came the paragraph she waited for:

"I always expected that we would get married when the war was over, without talking much about it. Here, I'm asking, Lindsey, will you marry me when I come home? I'll buy the Davis place for you. I remember how you took to that house. I'll take good care of you.

"I can't wait to come home, so that we can be together. Please write to me right away, Lindsey, and tell me your answer. I'll be waiting.

Love James"

Lindsey read his letter countless times; she soon knew it by heart. She wrote and re-wrote her reply. Each time she thought it dry, unfeeling, a poor picture of her ardor. In the end she wrote simply:

"Dear James:

Yes, I will marry you. I can't wait, either, till the war is over and you come home. We will get married and live forever in our own dear house, the two of us and our family. I will be the best wife to you that you could ever dream of. I promise, James.

All my love,

Lindsey"

She folded it carefully and slipped it into an envelope. She considered, holding the flap open, in case she should wish to add more endearments. At the end of the day she sealed it, deciding to let it go as it was, and propped it on her bedside table beside James' letter. She would take it first thing tomorrow to the post office. And she would tell her parents the wonderful news. "I love you, James." She kissed his letter and fell immediately into dreamless sleep.

Chapter Thirteen

Listening In

Lindsey spotted Miss Taylor in front of the mill one Saturday afternoon in late August as she left the telephone office. She was surprised to see her since school was not due to start for another week. She waved a greeting, and crossed the street.

"Miss Taylor, you're back early," she said.

"I'll have a few days to get settled in," Miss Taylor said. She was dressed in a navy skirt and a red striped shirt that emphasized the angular lines of her body. She wore sturdy shoes that made her look ready for a hike.

"How are you, Lindsey? Come walk along with me, we can get a Coke at Hedley's."

Without waiting for an answer she turned and started in that direction. Lindsey would have preferred to go on home. She had worked a double shift, and it had been constantly busy. Rather than try to explain she followed a half-pace behind as Miss Taylor strode on ahead and led the way to a booth in Hedley's dim back room.

"So this will be a big year for you," Miss Taylor said. "Your senior year, with decisions to make about what you will do after graduation."

"I'll work at the phone company for one more year to save money for college," Lindsey said. "Mrs. Simmons is retiring, and after graduation I will be working full-time."

"What do you hear from James?"

"He's still in camp, waiting for the war to be over so he can come home."

Lindsey had told no one except her parents, not even Barbara or Mrs. Cronkhite, about James' letter. She wanted James to come home first; she wanted to have all their plans in order before she made any announcements.

"And what will happen then, when he comes home?" Not for the first time Lindsey noticed how Miss Taylor's glasses magnified her eyes. She remembered how submitting to Miss Taylor's questions gave her that bug-under-a-microscope feeling.

"Well, of course he will go back to the farm." Lindsey said.

"And you will leave him on the farm and go off to college?"

"I have time to think about it," Lindsey said. She tried to keep the annoyance out of her voice.

"How are the Furlings getting along with James gone?" Miss Taylor changed the subject.

"I go and see Mrs. Furling, because I know she misses James. I never see Mr. Furling."

"Yes, he was always very busy," Miss Taylor nodded, and sucked up the last of her Coke.

"I'll get on back to the Bank's. They're expecting me for supper. I'll come out this evening to walk and catch up with friends from last year. I suppose I will see you? Or don't you come, now that James isn't here?"

"I do, I walk with Barbara."

She would prefer to stay home. But Barbara would be waiting for her in front of the phone company.

"Miss Taylor is here," she said later, as they met.

"Why did she come so early?" Barbara asked.

"I wondered."

They traversed the same familiar route, up on the river side of Main Street as far as the movie theater, back on the other side to the shops below the hotel.

Why are we doing this?

Lindsey half-listened to Barbara's chatter, remembering the pleasure she used to feel on a Saturday evening when she knew she would see James. She glimpsed Mr. Furling's pepper-and-salt slicked-back hair as they approached the station. He leaned on the brass rail where she had found James so many months before. He was in conversation with Mr. Davis, his neighbor, bending because Mr. Davis was a small man. Abruptly he broke off and straightened, looking in Lindsey's direction.

"So you are back," he said.

Lindsey thought for a moment he was speaking to her, but then heard Miss Taylor's voice behind her.

"For one more year," she said.

Miss Taylor always sounded school-marmish, Lindsey thought, even when she was being friendly. She and Barbara continued on. She could no longer hear their conversation.

* * * * * *

Now-a-days, until school started, Lindsey often worked the five-to-nine shift on Friday nights, a busy time, requiring two operators. It was the following Friday, mid-way through an afternoon shift, when the Furling flap went down.

"Number, please," she said briskly. She heard the smooth voice of James' dad, giving his request.

She stretched the companion cable to plug it into the Bank's number. Some time later she checked the sets of cables and disconnected those of conversations gone silent. As she checked the Furling cable she heard Mr. Furling's voice and stayed her hand.

"A trip to Rutland," he was saying. "Tomorrow, I need to get something. I think I'll have to take a little rest at that motel before starting back."

There was a ripple of laughter in reply. "What time do you figure that'd be?"

Lindsey's hand gripped the cord. The voice was as familiar to her as Mr. Furling's. She fought with disbelief, but she knew beyond doubting that it was Miss Taylor speaking.

"How about two?"

There was no answer, only the brief sound of another laugh before the click of the receiver.

Lindsey held the lever for another moment before she pulled the cords. She felt sick. She had heard the occasional ribald jokes of the other operators, making comments to each other about what they overheard. She had occasionally listened in to conversations in the late evening. It was idle entertainment; she did not know those people. To hear the voices of James' father and Miss Taylor's in response was like a blow.

After her shift was over, Lindsey went up-street to check their post office box. She knew there would likely be nothing from James but she wanted to delay going home. When she arrived there, her mother was at the stove, preparing their dinner.

"Mrs. Furling called," she looked up. "She said if you have time to come over tomorrow afternoon she'd love to see you. Mr. Furling has to go to Rutland on some errand."

"Yes," Lindsey said. "It will be a good time to see her. I'll go over at about two."

Chapter Fourteen

A Visit

The heat hung low over the river valley, as if September's first days had forgotten to change themselves from August. It welled up from the rough road and brought flies to hover over the cow patties. Lindsey kept her head down, careful to avoid the patties, walking along past the Furlings' barn toward their rambling farmhouse. The barnyard, empty, chopped and furrowed by the sharp hooves of the cattle, stretched back from the edge of the road waiting for the return of the herd.

When Lindsey reached the house, she stepped up onto the boulder that spanned two stones beside the kitchen porch. It teetered before she took the second step to the broad porch boards, where her feet made hollow echo.

The kitchen screen was immediately flung open and Mrs. Furling's broad figure filled the doorway. Her face gleamed with perspiration; she beamed as she wiped flour from her hands and arms with a damp dish cloth.

"Lindsey, I hoped you'd be able to come!" she exclaimed.

"I tried to call you."

"I was out picking peas. Knew I had to get 'em in so I could ready them today to put them up tomorrow."

"Can I help you?" she asked automatically, in no doubt of the answer.

"Why sure, you can shell them while I finish the biscuits." She led the way into the kitchen. An over-sized kitchen table, near the stove, covered with a red and white checked oilcloth was sprinkled liberally with trails of flour, and set about with bowls of dough.

"You know how it is at the end of the summer, everything comes at you at once that you have to get done before winter."

Lindsey dragged a kitchen chair to the end of the table. Mrs. Furling put a sack of peas on the floor and handed Lindsey a bowl. She then turned her attention then to the floury dough, slapping it into mounting white stacks.

They worked in silence. Lindsey came to see Mrs. Furling after James went off to the service, thinking she ought to get to know her better. What better way than to visit over cups of tea, as she did with Mrs. Cartwright? But Mrs. Furling had no time for tea. Lindsey doubted Mrs. Furling had ever taken an afternoon break in her whole life. No matter the season, she was overwhelmed with chores. To visit with Mrs. Furling was to share in her work.

Mrs. Furling battered the piles of dough into neat rounds. Taking a wet cloth she scrubbed the oilcloth of its incrustations of flour, and with another cloth dried it until it shone. She drew her chair next to Lindsey's so that they shared the sack of unshelled peas.

"What do you hear from James?" she asked. "Same as I do, I expect, that he is anxious to get home."

"He can't wait," Lindsey said.

They worked diligently. With Mrs. Furling's help, the peas pinged more often into the bowl. At last the sack was empty. Lindsey stretched her aching muscles. As she rose she felt the sweat trickling between her breasts and her skirt sticking to the backs of her legs.

"Let's sit out on the swing for a few minutes to cool off" she said. She filled two tumblers of water at the sink, handed one to Mrs. Furling and held the screen door open. In comparison to the kitchen the porch was cool and the swing was placed to catch the slight stir of air. They rocked it gently forth and back.

"It's good to set for a minute, isn't it?" Mrs. Furling said. "I should get out here more often."

Lindsey felt weighed down with knowledge. Sitting with Mrs. Furling in the swing, she forced herself to ignore what she knew.

"Mrs. Furling," she said with enormous effort. "When you and Mr. Furling were married, where did you go on your honeymoon?"

Lindsey saw Mrs. Furling's good-natured smile change to a look of surprise, and thought for a moment she had been too brash.

"Our honeymoon? Oh goodness, I haven't thought about that in so long."

She paused; her expression lost its habitual rictus of good nature and became dreamy, distant.

She is looking into the past.

"James' father and I were going together when I was in my last year of high school. He's a lot older than me, you know. I can tell you I was pretty set up to be keeping company with an older man. Made me feel special."

She laughed self-consciously, smoothing her skirt down over her knee. "His father had died when he was just a boy. He hardly remembers him, being the youngest. All his brothers and sisters had married and moved away and had their own places. So he was working the farm by himself, and looking after his mother. But she had a stroke of a sudden, and was bed-ridden. I was to go to nursing school that fall.

Instead, we got married and I came to take care of her. I did the best I could for her; she lived for eight years. So my honeymoon was in a room upstairs, same room as the one where we sleep now."

She paused again. "I remember so clear how it was, now that I think about it. It was late summer, the evenings were starting to get chill. There was a white quilt across the bed, the moonlight came in at the window and made the whole room white like early snow."

Mrs. Furling kicked her shoes off her swollen feet. She turned to look at Lindsey, her smile in place again. "A long time ago, that was! Lots of water has flowed under lots of bridges since then! Our wedding was a hurry-up affair, but I do have a wedding picture. You've seen it in on the mantel. My cousin loved to take pictures and she insisted we pose as if we were at a proper photographer."

Lindsey did indeed remember the picture. A round-faced young girl sat, smiling, ankles crossed, dressed in white, a bouquet across her arm. An older man stood, hand possessively on her shoulder. He was smiling slightly, not looking down at his bride, but gazing straight into the camera.

From the pose, Lindsey had thought it a picture of a previous generation. Mr. Furling, even though he was the older of the two, did not look much different, except that his dark hair was now streaked with gray. The young, open-faced girl in the picture was no longer recognizable.

"So I can't advise anyone on where to spend their honeymoon, Lindsey. We never got around to one. There never seemed to be time."

Chapter Fifteen

Change of Plans

August 6, 1945 began like any other day of the hot summer. Lindsey went to the phone company for the morning shift. By afternoon, the news came of the bomb dropped on Japan. In days, the war was miraculously over.

"They'll be coming home!" people who never spoke to their next-door neighbors called across the fences, smiling and waving. The men gathered at

Hedley's to drink late into the night. Within weeks, the boys and young men began to arrive home. One by one they returned from the places that the war had taken them. James had remained in the Florida training camp; he was home by mid-September. She was at the station to welcome him when he jumped down from the train, still in his uniform. It took her breath away to see him. In the year he had been gone—over a year—he had filled out; he was more handsome than she remembered. He gave her a quick, hard kiss, and turned to his hovering parents. Lindsey had to wait to see him alone; his cousins came from St. Johnsbury to welcome him back from the war. She had a brief evening with him in the truck, hours when she led her parents to think they had gone to the movies. She was left trembling, overwhelmed with happiness. Each day he spent with his father going about to see the changes in the farm, talking about its future. Lindsey was nagged with regret that there seemed so little time to discuss their own plans.

She worked her shifts at the phone company, fending off questions about James, knowing that her co-workers were curious. After lunch one day, she could stand it no longer; she walked over to the Furlings', calculating the time of her visit. She helped Mrs. Furling at her chores in the kitchen, distracted, listening for the cowbells in the mountain pasture. At last they tolled, muffled, then mingling with the heavy thudding of the hooves in the path rounding the house. James' whistle shrilled as they reached the barnyard gate. She knew he would come then, for a brief time before the milking, and strained to hear his step on the porch.

"Lindsey." James' face lighted up as he came in.

He passed behind her to go to the long sink, letting his hand trail across her bare neck. He ran a tumbler of water and drank deeply, then cupped his hands in the running water and, bending, splashed his face. He smoothed his wet hands over his hair, and pulled the roller towel to pat the dripping water away.

"Hot for September," he said. "It's like I'm still in Florida."

He ran another tumbler of water, and one for Lindsey, indicating with a nod of his head the door to the porch.

"Come take a break,"

"Go, go," said Mrs. Furling. "I'm going to run up to the barn and look for a few eggs."

Lindsey waited for James to speak as they sat in the corner swing.

"So, Lindsey," he said. "When's the wedding?"

She was startled by his directness. "I couldn't plan it until you got here."

"Well, now I'm here; you can go ahead." James shook his head, leaned back and stretched his arms. "I don't know how Dad has been keeping up with the farm, even with Randy helping out."

"James, forget the farm for a minute. You can't just say 'Go plan the wedding.' There's a lot we have to talk about. Like where will we go for our honeymoon? Where will we live when we come back?"

James nodded, but continued with his own thoughts. "There's so much work to catch up on that

Dad hasn't been able to do," he frowned. "You remember us talking about the Davis place, up the hill?"

"Oh yes, the house!" Lindsey had seen the Davis place many times since she had been there with James years ago. She had imagined herself in it, had remembered James saying he meant to have that farm one day. "What about it, James?"

"He's sick, can't farm any more, they're finally selling out."

Her heart leaped in her chest. "But would we have enough to buy?"

"I got cash from the Army. Enough for a good down payment, especially since they're going to keep the house."

Lindsey broke in. "They are going to keep the house? What do you mean?"

"Just that," James said. He waved his hand. "One of the daughters and her husband want to take over the house, with one lot, but got no interest in the land."

"Oh, I am so sorry." Lindsey tried to ignore her distress. "I loved that house so much. But do you still want to buy it if there is no place for us to live?"

James turned to face her, "I've been thinking. Dad and I been talking about it. The Davis farm would give us about twice the fields we have. With a good tractor we could handle it. You can't run a farm with a team of horses any more, that's over. I got enough money for a down payment, and for a good tractor."

"But we still need a place to live," Lindsey said.

"I been thinking about that too, just last night." James said. "This will work out even better. We can live right here. We can fix up one of those big rooms upstairs. No sense to find another place to live. I'd be right here, ready to start work. We could save lots of money and pay off the farm, make improvements. It's perfect, Lindsey, much better than if we had the house."

Lindsey needed time to think; she felt suddenly that everything was moving much too fast.

"James," she said, putting her hand on his knee. "Let's think about this. Do your parents know that you want to move us in here? That you want to have us living upstairs?"

"They'd think it was a great idea," James said, his face intent. "Me and Dad would have to work hard, but together we could do it. Ma would have a lot of work too, but you'd be here."

James smiled down at her. "Besides helping Ma with the work, you'd be keeping each other company."

Lindsey heard the kitchen door open. Mrs. Furling was back from the barn with the eggs.

"James, please, before you talk to them, let's think about it,"

His face clouded. "If you want, but not for long."

Mrs. Furling came around the corner of the porch, holding her apron out. "They been laying real well this week. I'll make a package to send some home with you."

"It's time for you to start the milking," Lindsey said to James. She was glad of the interruption. She wanted to go home, to postpone more discussion. She thanked Mrs. Furling for the eggs, and followed James out to walk with him until they parted at the barn.

He pulled her to him and kissed her. She smelled the sweat of his farm work; the back of his shirt was still damp. "Don't worry, Lindsey. It's going to be work out fine."

"Yes," she said.

But why wasn't she convinced?

Chapter Sixteen

More Change of Plans

Lindsey walked home rapidly, in spite of the heat, over the lower bridge up Main Street. Her parents were seated in the living room. She threw herself into one of the chairs. Her face was flushed.

"James wants me to plan the wedding. That's what he said today. The sooner the better, he said." Lindsey got the words out before she bent over and covered her face to hide her tears. She had held them in while she listened to James, and while she walked home, but now they poured down her cheeks.

"Baby, whatever is it? That should make you happy." Her mother's face showed her concern. "Did you and James quarrel? What is wrong, dear?"

"No, no." Lindsey gasped.

"Then what is it? What's the matter?" Her dad was embarrassed. Sensing his unease helped Lindsey regain control.

"James has gone out of his mind," she said. "He's got this great idea that he will buy the Davis place we always wanted, he's got enough saved to make a down payment, and he will take the rest of his money from the Army and buy a big tractor so that they would be able to work it."

"That doesn't sound like a bad idea," her dad said.

"Mom, Dad, let me tell you! That money was supposed to go for a down payment on a house for us on our own place. You remember when I talked about the Davis place up the road from the Furlings, I told you about the house there, but they don't want to sell the house, only the land. James doesn't even talk about us having our own place. He talks about his dad's place as if he's going to be there the rest of his life—the rest of our lives."

Lindsey struggled for coherency.

"He thinks it will be a great idea for us to live in a room upstairs in that awful farmhouse! I couldn't bear it. You haven't been up there – they're just big barns of plain old rooms. He talks about painting them and fixing them up; but I know he never would. They never do anything about that house; it's practically falling apart. Any money they get goes to fix up the barn. They never get around to doing anything about the house. It's just the farm and the cows and the pigs that are important."

The tears welled up again. Lindsey clenched her fists.

"And that's not all. The reason he thinks this is such a great idea is that we could be right there to work all the time. He wouldn't waste any time, he said: he could start the minute he woke up and work till dark. We'd never do anything; I know, I've seen how they do; all they do is work."

"Of course that's what farm life is, Lindsey."

"And he even said, yes, get this, it would be nice for me too, that I would be helping his mother, we'd be keeping each other company."

"You always said you liked Mrs. Furling," her mother said.

"I like her well enough, but to spend all my time with her? All day, every day? We don't have much to talk about, you know. It's not like having tea with Mrs. Cartwright in the library talking about books and what's going on in the world. Its work, work, work, doing dumb things like cutting up beans and shelling peas, and worse things like making blood sausage and other disgusting things when they slaughter the pigs."

"Did you tell James how you felt about moving in with his parents?"

"I didn't get a chance. He was going on like it was the most wonderful idea and that nobody in their right mind could possibly disagree. He was like someone possessed. I just listened and didn't say anything. I was afraid I'd start to cry."

"Tomorrow you go see him and tell him how you feel. If he knows you are so upset he won't insist; you can work it out."

"Work it out! You just showed how little you know James, Mama. When he gets an idea in his head, it takes hold of him. He can't imagine any other way of thinking, especially if it's about that farm."

Lindsey calmed herself enough to eat. As soon as she had helped her mother to clear the table and wash the dishes, she went up to her room. She tried to be done with crying, but the tears dripped down her cheeks. How could she describe to James what she wanted, when he never asked her? She was assailed by such a jumble of feelings that she could not sort them out. How would they ever come to an understanding of each other? How could it ever come right?

Chapter Seventeen

At The Farm

Lindsey wakened the next morning unrefreshed from a restless night. The weight of disappointment pressed in on her, like an animal held at bay by sleep, waiting to pounce in the first waking moment. She spent the day at the telephone company working mechanically, wanting to see James, waiting for his call.

"Did you hear from James today?" her mother asked, before they ate.

Lindsey admitted she had not. "I work early shift tomorrow," she said. "I'll go over there after that."

It was noon when she walked across the lower bridge toward the Furling farm. She expected to have a session with Mrs. Furling before she had a chance to talk to James. But as she passed the barn James called to her, and came out to meet her.

"The folks are gone," he told her. "Dad's uncle up in St. Johnsbury took a bad turn, they had to get up there to help. Likely they'll be back tomorrow."

Randy had been lending him a hand with the milking, he went on to explain.

The sun shone as it had in the days before, but now there was a persistent wind, a reminder that it was no longer summer.

"Let's get in and have some lunch,"

Lindsey followed James to the house. His expression was smooth, untroubled, reflecting nothing of her own tumult. In the kitchen the banked fire in the cook-stove gave off a pleasant warmth. He lifted the front lid and stirred the embers with the poker before he fed in another chunk of wood.

James fetched plates and cutlery from the cupboards and set them out on the corner of the long kitchen table. Though she had been so many times in the Furling house it was the first time she had been alone there with James.

We have to talk.

James said "Ma baked bread yesterday, and there's cheese, and sliced ham. We can have a real good lunch."

After lunch then, we have to talk.

James cut the freshly baked bread on the wooden board, and laid out slices of cheese and ham. She brought the butter from the shelf beside the ice box and spread it thickly on the slices of bread. He moved the coffee pot from the back of the stove onto a front burner.

She half-listened while he talked about what he had done with the fields and what his dad had found out about tractors. They finished eating and she poured them mugs of coffee.

Now. This is the time.

As she was about to speak. James rose and put his drained coffee mug in the sink. "If you're finished your coffee let's go upstairs. I can show you that room."

He waited, standing, while she took her last sip of coffee. Obediently she followed him to the staircase in the hall and they mounted to the second floor, their steps echoing in the empty house.

How quiet it is without Mrs. Furling here.

"The rooms that get the most sun are on this side." James said, as they walked the corridor. "This one next to Ma and Dad's, then the one down on the end. It's more private."

He went on to the farther one, pushing open the last door. It creaked slightly as it swung back. The room was empty of furniture. The double dormer windows opposite the door, uncurtained and needing washing, looked out on the path leading down from the mountain and around the end of the house. A large braided rug, its muted colors faded, took up much of the painted floor. On the left there was a large wooden clothes closet.

"Not fancy, but once it's furnished, with curtains and all," James said. "There's some white paint up at the barn would freshen it up."

They stood side by side, next to each other, looking out the windows. He turned his head to look down at her, waiting.

He wants me to like it.

She put her hand on his elbow. "It's not that it wouldn't be nice, James."

He heard the doubt in her voice; she saw the disappointment on his face.

"It isn't like we'd be moving in with strangers," he said. "We'd be at home."

"Your home, not our home,"

"Just for a few years, while we were getting started. Then we could get our own place."

James would be happy enough. He would go out every day to work the land with his dad. Despite his well-meant promises he would not be impelled to move on.

I'll get old here. I'll be like Mrs. Furling.

Year after year in a house that wasn't her own, making do in a room with double dormer windows that looked out on a path up the mountain.

"You never cared that much for the Davis house, so you don't care about losing it." Lindsey knew before she finished speaking that she had thrown up a wall between herself and James. With her words his face was a mix of emotions, willfulness love, anger. In a moment they passed away, he looked stubborn, like a child.

"If I didn't care it's because it isn't important. A house is a house. It's the land that matters."

He saw the hurt in her face; his expression changed again to contrition. He put his arm around her shoulders.

"We'll work it out. We'll find a way."

"Yes," she said. "We'll find a way."

In silence they went back down to the kitchen. Tidying up, they talked of unimportant things. It was the hour for James to tend to the cows.

Lindsey walked with him as far as the barn, raising her cheek for his kiss. She allowed herself a moment to feel optimistic, thinking of his promises.

But he isn't going to change.

It did not matter what he promised. She knew she would be the one who would do the changing.

Chapter Eighteen

Lindsey's Parents

"Did you talk to James, Lindsey?" her mother called from the kitchen as she came home. Her father sat at the desk in the living room.

"No. Tomorrow." Lindsey knew her mother was waiting for an explanation. "The Furlings weren't there. They had to drive up north to take care of a relative. They will be back tomorrow."

"But James was there," her mother came in and looked at her curiously.

"Yes, he was. He was busy."

Lindsey did not want to talk about James. She wanted to be by herself, to avoid questions. "I'm tired." she said. "I'll be working tonight; I better go take a nap."

She noticed the pile of maps on the desk as she turned to go. "What's all that?"

"Dad and I have been considering what to do," her mother said.

"Do? About what?"

Her dad pushed the desk chair back, and turned towards her. "Won't be long until all these boys will be coming home," he said. "Ed Sherman's got two sons and a half dozen nephews. He can take any of 'em into the business and pay them a fraction of what he's paying me."

"But you'll find something else,"

"There won't be many jobs around here."

"We are thinking about Florida. Dad would like to see what he could find down there," her mother said.

"Florida! Why Florida?"

Lindsey had never considered them leaving. She had pictured their lives continuing on in more or less the same fashion after she married James.

"There's going to be a lot of new business there. Those boys who have been in the training camps, a lot of them will settle down there, start families."

"And it doesn't snow in Florida," her mother said. "We're tired of snow. We want to be where it's warm."

They're outsiders here. That's the real reason.

"We wouldn't leave until you are settled down with James, of course," her mother said. "I'll help you with the wedding."

"It will be strange without you," Lindsey said. "I'll be alone here."

"But you'll have James," her mother said.

Her dad gathered up the stack of maps and slipped a rubber band around them. "The other day I passed Cal Shaw across from the school when I was walking to work. He said, 'We want to invite you folks over for a game of cards some night.' He's been saying that to me at least once a week for the last three years. I said, 'Any time. We been waiting quite a few years now.'"

"Oh, Daddy, how rude!"

"He's the one who's rude. The way he looked I guess no one ever pointed it out to him before. Sometimes you have to just come out and say it."

Her dad thought for a moment, and nodded his head. "I'll have a talk with Ed when I go in tomorrow. Best to get it all out in the open."

"Yes," her mother said. "When things are out in the open you can tell which way you want to go." She stepped closer to her husband, smiling at him as she slipped her arm around his waist.

Lindsey's chest felt heavy, but before she went upstairs she forced herself to be calm.

They are outsiders, but they know what they want.

In her small room, she was swept by a torrent of feelings. She tried to sort them out. It was impossible, they bubbled up to the surface, her feeling of calm deserted her. As on so many other evenings she took out the box which held the locket that James had given her, and rubbed the nubby velvet against her cheek. She slipped the chain over her head and turned out the light. She wished she were a child again so that someone could tell her what to do.

Chapter Nineteen

Fire

Lindsey slept fitfully and dreamed of James, longing for him. She awakened in the half-light of dawn. She imagined the faint odor of burning, before dozing off once more. Then she awoke with a start. The smell of smoke was sharp and strong. In that moment, she heard the bell at the fire station tolling, and shouts from the street below.

Oliver Gist, on his way to his early shift at the mill, had been the first to note the smell of smoke. He couldn't tell where it was coming from, he told his listeners later, repeating his story over and over. He walked through the mill, looking for fire, he said, and then, out the back window that opened onto the river, saw the pall of smoke growing over the school. He rushed to call the operator at the phone company telling her to rouse the volunteer firemen. The grey smoke over the school increased. He called her again to say she better call Ransom and Rutland for extra help.

Lindsey dressed hurriedly and was on the street at the same time as the first truck left the fire house. The siren screamed its rolling call as the truck pulled to the top of the bridge. The firemen attached the hose to the fire hydrant on the curb and wrestled it into position. The hose straightened and filled, the stream of water spat sporadically, gathered force, and belched clots of water from the nozzle. Two men hauled it upright. The stream arched up, wavering, reaching the second floor of the school. It played down the front wall, glistening on the windows, dripping from the eaves.

"She's a goner," someone near Lindsey said. A crowd was gathering.

Despite the water, the flames licked at the dry wood, charring the paint, penetrating the eaves, leaping from crevice to crevice.

"Where's Gimpy?" she cried out. The people around her looked at her curiously.

Flames flickered darkly through the glass-panel side-lights of the wide front door. There was no way that Gimpy could escape through the cat door beneath the side panel. He would retreat to the second floor attempting to get away from the heat.

More people arrived to stand in the parking lot, and in the street. The men pushed forward to try and help; the firemen gave them instructions, shouting to be heard above the noise.

The Ransom firetruck pulled into the lot. They had loaded all the hose they had; they were able to reach the hydrant at the foot of the bridge. After a shouted discussion among them, the second crew set up their hose to turn streams of water on the White Church next door and on the Shaw and Preston houses across the street. The crowd of women and children were harried from place to place by the firemen as they dragged the hose.

"They got to keep the fire from spreading down the block," said someone in the crowd.

James and his father moved about amongst the men up front. Lindsey's dad and all the men were trying to help.

"Look, Jud's going up," someone shouted. A limping figure mounted the fire escape, pausing on each rung. The janitor, dragging his bad leg, his hand on the inner rail, pulled an axe behind him with his other hand as he went up.

Jud reached the top platform of the fire escape. He leaned back against the railing and raised the axe above his head. He brought it down on the narrow door that led into the school. The door held firm, he struck at it again and again. It cracked and gave way, its pieces crashing inward. Smoke poured from the jagged opening. Jud drew back for a moment from the smoke that poured out and then pushed his way through. Several men ran up the fire escape after him. Before they reached the top Jud came out of the broken door.

Lindsey's mother had come, and was standing at her elbow.

"Mom, look, he's got Gimpy!"

Through the smoke the cat's orange fur was a fuzzy blur against Jud's dark shirt. He was hanging half on Jud's shoulder, and half on his chest. Jud's one hand held to Gimpy's back as he turned to go down the iron steps. He kept to the railing, stopping every few steps to reach back for the axe.

"He did it, Mom! He brought Gimpy out," Lindsey felt the tears wet on her cheeks; she could not help herself.

Everyone in town was there now. Barbara stood with her mother. Miss Taylor was alone, her hair twisted up in a blood-red bandana, her glasses—two pools of smoky scarlet—reflected the flames. The chatter and cries of the onlookers rose and fell and rose again as the clouds of smoke issued from the upper door. Another truck arrived from Rutland, with tanks of water. The driver crossed the lot and drew up close to the school. Its hoses played steadily on the walls of the lower floors. The big glass windows streamed with water; the ground around the building turned into mud.

Mr. Furling stood with a knot of men beside one hose, with James nearby. Mrs. Furling held to Mrs. Davis' arm on the curb with a group of women. Her own father stood stiffly near the new hoses with the Rutland firemen. .

There was a discussion later about what time the roof fell in. Some said noon, but the fireman from Ransom had looked at his watch just then and said it was eleven twenty when it collapsed, sending a shower of sparks down on the parking lot. It was a Fourth of July celebration crazily out of control. People slapped at the embers that drifted down on their hair and on their clothing. The fire trucks continued pouring water on the burning walls. The firemen stamped on nests of embers fallen on dry ground. People were quiet now, staring at the wreckage, their faces flushed, intent.

They are thrilled to be here.

They would say to each other for years to come, 'Were you there that day the school burned down?'

James and his father dragged a hose across a patch of wet ground searching for dry spots where the fire might erupt again. Silhouetted against the ruined building each of them leaned slightly backwards, grasping the thick hose between them. *How similar they are, like a cut-out.*

Lindsey noticed again that they were copies of each other, father and son.

Her mother plucked at her sleeve. "We might as well go home," she said. "There's nothing more we can do here."

Lindsey looked across at James. He gestured at what remained of the school, in conversation with a Rutland fireman.

"Yes," she said. "It's finished here."

Chapter Twenty

Change of Heart

Lindsey noticed the difference in the air as soon as she stepped outside to walk to the telephone company that night. The odor of burning hung thickly over the town. No breeze stirred. The smoke drifted above the river and along the streets, clinging to clothing, clogging the lungs, its pungent smell made sharper by the evening dampness. Lights shone dully on the bridge and above in the schoolyard.

Volunteers watched to see that the fire did not erupt again. Their voices, muted by the river, echoed indistinctly in the darkness.

"You'll be busy," the evening operator said. "Everyone wants to talk about the fire."

Lindsey had no time to think as she connected and disconnected the cables. She worked steadily. It was almost eleven o'clock before the calls became more sporadic. She watched for the Furling flap to go down. It was later than usual when she heard it fall and James answered her careful, "number, please."

"I volunteered," James said, "I'll go at midnight or one and help watch through the night. To make sure it doesn't flare up again."

"I could hear them when I came over," she said. She was drained of feeling, exhausted by the events of the long day.

"I can come over to see you before I go up there," he said.

"Of course," she said, "I'll leave the door open." Her voice sounded dull and flat to her own ears.

Lindsey unlatched the chain lock while continued to answer calls. In a few minutes he came, bringing in with him a wave of dampness and woodsmoke. He bent quickly to kiss her, rubbing his rough cheek against her neck, shrugging off his jacket and throwing it across the rail.

"They been talking about replacing the old school for a long time." James said, "Now they'll have to do it." He talked excitedly about the events of the day even though she had witnessed them, too. At last she broke in.

"James," she said, to claim his attention, "I've been thinking. Maybe we should wait a while before we get married."

He stared at her. "Lindsey, what the hell are you saying? I been waiting for two years. Wait for what?"

Lindsey's courage ebbed. "I'm just not sure any more," she said.

"But you were sure," he said. His voice was hard and flat. "What's this all about?"

James' face set into harsh lines.

He's not sad, he's angry

"I know what it is," he said, "you wanted to have the Davis house, that's what changed your mind, isn't it? It was always the house, not us."

"You promised," she said, "and then you didn't care."

"It's just a damn house," he said. The bitterness in his voice matched the bitterness in her heart. "A house doesn't matter."

He doesn't understand.

Lindsey knew that whatever she might say James would never understand. More than that, she could not understand him, either. She got up from her stool, and faced him. She put her hand to her neck, hooking her fingers in the thin chain that held the locket. With one motion she pulled it over her head and held it out to him. It swung between them, first to her and then towards him, twisting on the dangling chain. Her tears welled up, but she willed herself not to cry.

"Here, take this back," she said, "I'm sorry, I am really sorry."

Part Three

Twinbridge Farewell

1975

Lindsey found her husband still sleeping when she returned to the B&B from her walk around Twinbridge. Scott was a slow starter in the mornings—a good thing he hadn't been a farmer—she could not imagine him getting up to do early morning chores. While he dressed she called her sister-in-law, who was minding the children in Jersey. Mitzi was to deliver them to scout camp this morning; there might be some last minute questions.

"No, absolutely no candy in their backpacks." she said. "Pay no attention to what the children are telling you. The camp counselors were very clear about that."

At the last minute, although he was already dressed, Scott decided to change from his plain blue button-down shirt to a seer-sucker stripe. She ignored his muttered comments about looking right when he met her old boyfriends.

"Don't fuss," she said. "No one is going to be dressed up."

She herself had given considerable thought about what to wear to the Reunion Luncheon at the White Church. She had selected a mini-skirted dress with a sweetheart neckline, suitable for the occasion and flattering to her still-slim figure. She found shoes that had only a suggestion of platform soles so that she would not be too much taller than Scott.

"Come, let's take a walk," she said when they had finished dressing. "We have time before the lunch. I'll show you the town."

Lindsey did not tell her husband that she had already walked through town. He had slept so soundly he had not missed her. Together they retraced the steps she had taken earlier. She pointed out to him the White Church, the park where the school had been, and the other landmarks of her youth. She showed him the window of the old post office and described how the mail sacks were unloaded from the afternoon train and carried across the street. They continued on, past the small park beside the railroad station toward the plain rectangular building which had housed the movie theater.

"Redemption Center?" Scott said. "Are they having a religious revival?"

He stared at the tower now attached to the end of the building. From the top of it down, black capital letters faced the street, spelling R-E-D-E-M-P-T-I-O-N. She herself was for a moment confused, then realized its meaning.

"Everyone saves those little green stamps they give you at the grocery stores," she said. "You paste them in books, and when you have enough pages you redeem them. This is where you come to get your prizes."

"Jesus, what an eyesore."

She must keep him from making comments about the Redemption Center should the subject come up at lunch. They crossed Main Street and she showed him the Library. Slowly they made their way back, past the bank, the fire station, the Town Hall and up over the bridge to the White Church.

Lindsey saw James the moment they entered the Social Hall. Beside him was a woman dressed in a nondescript skirt and blouse. She was startled to realize that it was Barbara. No one had told her. Why would they?

How worn she looks.

James wore a blue button-down shirt; thank heaven Scott had changed to the seer-sucker. She and Scott moved toward their group; she breathed deeply to right herself. Unfamiliar-looking people milled about. Schoolmates she could no longer recognize, or spouses she had never met? The day was warm; the color in her cheeks would pass unnoticed. She was greeted by name by a heavy woman she did not remember. The voice, though, stirred memory. Margaret used to sit in back of her in class; her voice had not changed.

"Margaret," she said. "How good to see you again."

"You finally came back to visit us," Margaret said. "We always wondered what became of you after you graduated and left town with your folks."

Margaret pulled at Barbara's sleeve, and Barbara turned from James' side. "Barbara, look who's here. It's Lindsey."

"Finally," Lindsey said, "we were able to get back to a reunion."

Barbara let go of James' arm and faced her.

"Oh, Lindsey I had no idea you would be here today," Barbara smiled with genuine pleasure. She was missing a side front tooth; she put a hand to her mouth. "We didn't know what happened to you all these years."

Lindsey felt called to account and the color mounted to her cheeks. "I went to Florida with my parents."

"Is that where you have been all this time?"

Barbara's and Margaret's round faces were absorbed as they stood together watching her. James watched too, and listened. A silence fell in the group around them. She hurried to answer, tripping over her words.

"I went to Florida with them, but I didn't stay there long. I went to New York."

Barbara nodded. "You used to say you wanted to go to New York."

"I didn't stay there long either. I met Scott." She had met Scott in the office where she worked. It had been a slow courtship, Scott was stiff and studious, and not given, in those days, to small talk. Of course she was not going to go into all that.

"We got married and Scott got a job overseas, and that's where we've been until now, in different places abroad."

Enough about me.

"But Barbara, tell me how you've been. You look great." Lindsey said. She was embarrassed by her lie, and was relieved to see that it was accepted complacently.

"James and I were married a year after you left," Barbara said. She nodded again, a prideful look on her face.

"And the farm, how is the farm?"

How inane.

"James has done real well with both the farms," Barbara said, "and we fixed up the big house real nice. You must come see us."

"We must," Lindsey said, knowing they would not.

"I'm sorry you didn't get to see James' ma. She passed a year ago."

And you took care of her in her old age.

The silence around them eased, talk began again. Her conversation with Barbara over, Lindsey moved closer to James. She had thought him unchanged, as she saw him from across the room. He did not have the pot belly that she had begun to notice in her own husband. Standing close, she saw he was slightly stooped, his shoulders less broad, his body gaunt. His hand, when he shook hers, was hard and calloused. She turned to include Scott, but he had left her side. He had gone on ahead, moving from group to group, chatting, turning on the charm in the way he had learned to do at parties.

She looked back at James, at James and Barbara standing together. The men who had been their classmates stood around them in a shuffling circle.

"Not often you take a day off from the farm," one of them said. Since James stood taller than the others, his head well above the rest, Lindsey saw his face clearly. His face wrinkled in amusement as he glanced down at Barbara, he said something to her and they all laughed. Barbara touched his elbow, looking up at him. Lindsey felt tears welling up in response to bittersweet memories, and took a deep breath.

Only twenty-five years.

Where was Scott? She missed him for a moment, but caught sight of his seer-sucker shirt, his back turned to her. Having made the rounds, he stood awkwardly near the table looking about for someone—anyone—with whom to talk. She stepped forward and linked her arm through his. She felt calmed, as if after the passing of a storm.

"Let's not stay any longer than we have to, after the lunch," she said. "We have a long drive ahead. I can't wait to get home."

The End

Made in the USA
Lexington, KY
03 May 2018